Amanda S. Mosaic

THE MAKING OF
MY SNOWMAN

My Snowman goes on a journey

My Snowman goes on a journey
(Colour your Storybook)

My Snowman enjoys the summer

My Snowman enjoys the summer
(Colour your Storybook)

My Snowman at the Maker Faire

My Snowman at the Maker Faire
(Colour your Storybook)

The Making Of… My Snowman

ISBN: 978-3-948493-13-4

It's been a long, long time today,
Since I made plans to go away,

To travel to far distant lands,
The money though was not at hand.

The job I had was very small,
It did not pay enough at all!

And this is how it all began:
With day-dreams and a crazy plan.

TERRANOVA
NEW YORK
WASHINGTON
OZEAN
ATLANTIK
RABAT
ALGERIEN
SAHARA
BAHAMAS
DOMINIKANISCHE
REPUBLIK
PUERTO RICO
SANTO
DOMINGO
JAMAIKA
NICARAGUA
MANAGUA
PANAMA
CARACAS
VENEZUELA
BOGOTA
KOLUMBIEN
GUYANA
SURINAM
FRANZ.-GUYANA
BRASILIEN
40°

I needed something I could sell,
A treat, I thought, would do quite well.

A simple treat was not enough,
I wanted bigger, better stuff!

My treat was made of gingerbread,
Not just a man, a house instead.

The icing holds it all in place,
The roof as well as Snowman's face.

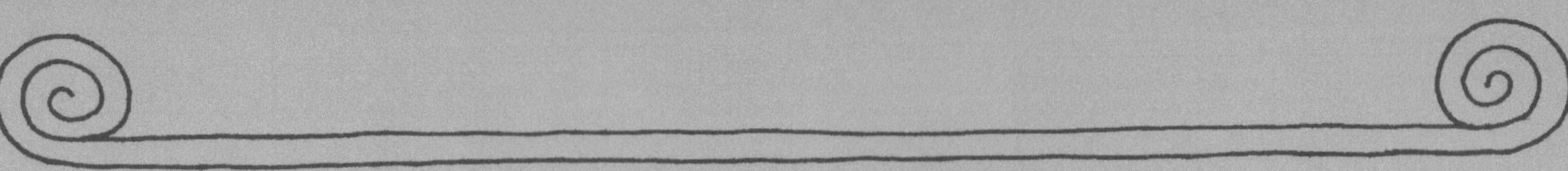

My Snowman is not made of snow.
I was afraid he'd melt, you know.

But coconut is white as well.
An awesome choice, he's looking swell.

His eyes are sweet brown chocolate chips.
He holds a dark brown chocolate stick.

Two biscuits make a proper hat,
Another one the welcome mat.

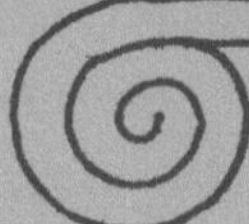

The first house is completely done.
My Snowman smiles and I had fun.

But I need more than one house only.
And surely Snowman would be lonely!

So, on to building number two,
It needs a tree and sprinkles, too!

Soon I have a little hamlet,
Still I am not really done yet!

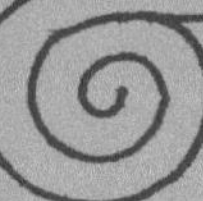

The last house here is pretty small;
Had only scraps to build it all.

There is no Snowman on the grounds,
It's more a shed with trees around.

A deep blue well and crocodile,
Make it a special domicile.

I think, I'll keep this one for me,
I'd like to have a house for free.

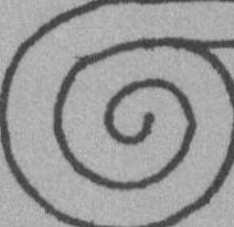

It's time to take a little rest.
I don't know which one I like best,

They all look pretty sweet and nice:
It looks like Candy Paradise!

Let's count… how many did I make,
Before I took this well-earned break?

Sixteen houses deck the table.
I wrap them all. Do they need labels?

The houses sold out very fast.
No wonder, none of them did last:

My Snowman was the obvious star,
He made my houses popular.

Soon after I did book the flight,
The journey was a real delight.

This trip I fondly will remember;
It kept me baking all November.

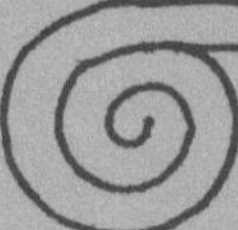

The Snowman soon did disappear.
I no more thought of him, my dear.

A new plan was not yet in sight,
My Snowman's quiet, sitting tight.

No single word in eight long years,
When suddenly he reappeared:

The blank book my friend offered me,
Made sure I wrote it down, you see:

My Gingerbread Home(s)
(12 Bilder -> Kalender daraus machen.)
Mikado
North America
Radler?
Polar Zone
Radler
Africa
Trailer
Castle
Schneebal (Grad A)
Grabstein
R.I.P.
In Kiste mit Deckel angelehnt
Boot
Festn...
Ein Schneemann stand tagein, tagaus,
vor meinem kleinen Lebkuchenhaus.
Doch eines Morgens, ach, oh Schreck!
Da war der Schneemann plötzlich weg!
Wurd' er entführt oder gestohlen?
War's gut, die Polizei zu holen?
als vermisst gemeldet
... aber nicht beendet
Vielleicht ist er auch blaß entla...
Nun unterwegs, um ein zukaufe...
Ich find' ihn nicht, er bleibt v...
Vielleicht wollt' er die Welt erku...
Rom Paris
WELT
Ob Tokio, New York, Athen,
da gibt es wirklich viel zu seh'n.
Ach, hätt' er mich doch mitgenommen,
ich wär' so gerne mitgekommen.
Mein Schneemann
VERMISST!
MISSING!
My Snowman

The Poem I had on my mind,
Would not get lost nor left behind.

This winter Snowman did return,
But just for fun and not to earn.

He was the Hero of my lines.
He made us laugh out many times.

Years would pass from poem to story,
From early draft to final glory.

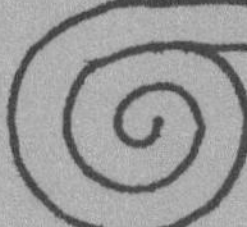

And this was only half the book,
New pictures would complete the look.

My ideas are really boundless,
I will make much more than houses!

Castles, pyramids and igloos,
Horses… – oh, the list continues!

Now, I can't wait to make it real,
My vision has such great appeal!

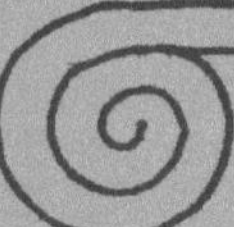

The pyramid is such a feat;
The angles are just right, indeed!

With palm trees all around the base
And camels – it's a lovely place.

I move on to the second piece
And suddenly I'm ill at ease:

It does not go as I had planned.
Why is it getting out of hand?

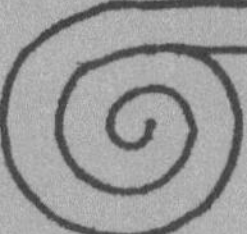

That Snowman does not look like mine!
I try a lot and then resign.

I could not find more chocolate chips
And therefore now the rest won't fit!

Blue icing has a strange effect
And did not work as I'd expect.

I let it go, set up the rest,
Then grab my camera for a test.

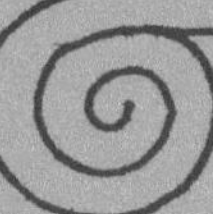

I had not really thought it through:
The weather was a challenge too!

It turned out to be way too hot,
To take that single perfect shot.

The chocolate melts, the guitar breaks,
The heat puts everything at stake!

But should I wait another season?
Of course, I suddenly feel beaten.

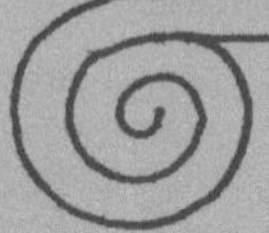

I figured not and soon discovered
That I could draw what once did bother.

I now had many chocolate chips,
My pen would do this magic trick.

I liked my Snowman so much better;
The weather did no longer matter.

And soon I have a picture ready,
The book is growing very steady.

I make a book for colouring
With only outlines I begin.

I'll make a second version too:
A storybook to read to you.

But just not yet, it takes some time,
Much more, you know, than did the rhyme.

In the end I will have twenty.
For a small book that is plenty.

I love the pictures and the text.
I guess you know what I do next:

I ask someone to print it all
And turn it into books for all.

Once I have a printed copy,
I feel proud and really happy.

Soon I gave it as a present
To my cousin who was pregnant.

The pencils come in many hues,
Which one of them did I most use?

The light blue is the shortest one,
There's lots of sky around the sun.

I used the dark and lighter green
For all the plants that can be seen.

Well, I used more than green and blue.
What else is in the pictures too?

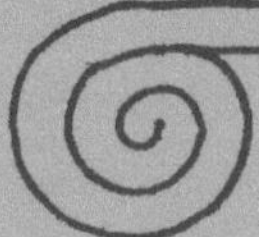

OF SWITZERLAND
FANCOLOR

Then I wrote a few more books
And this is how their covers look.

From time to time I choose to send,
A book as gift to a dear friend.

Sometimes they really live close by,
Sometimes my parcel has to fly.

My parents are already set,
My brother does not have one yet.

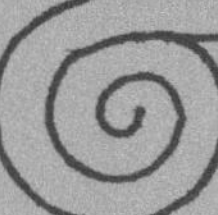

CHNEEMANN
AKER FAIRE
Mosaic

MEIN SCHNEEMANN
HAT SOMMERFERIEN
Amanda S. Mosaic

MEIN SCHNEE
GEHT AUF RE
Amanda S. M

NWMAN
R FAIRE

MY SNOWMAN
ENJOYS THE SUMMER
Amanda S. Mosaic

MY SNOW
GOES ON A J
Aman

I don't know if they still remember
The stories made up in my chamber.

I doubt that I have shared them all,
My mind held many, big and small.

Now I am grown-up, I can write,
New stories fill my mind at night.

If you, my dear, have stories too,
I know a thing that you can do:

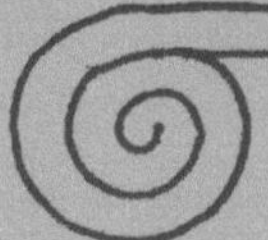

Just grab a pen and get a paper
And draw or write – I'll see you later…

Then store it in a special place,
One day, this treasure might amaze.

Joleen did draw this one for me.
I saw it and I squealed with glee.

Now tell me, what would Snowman do,
If he had time to visit You?

EXTRAS

1
2
3
4
5
6
7
8
9

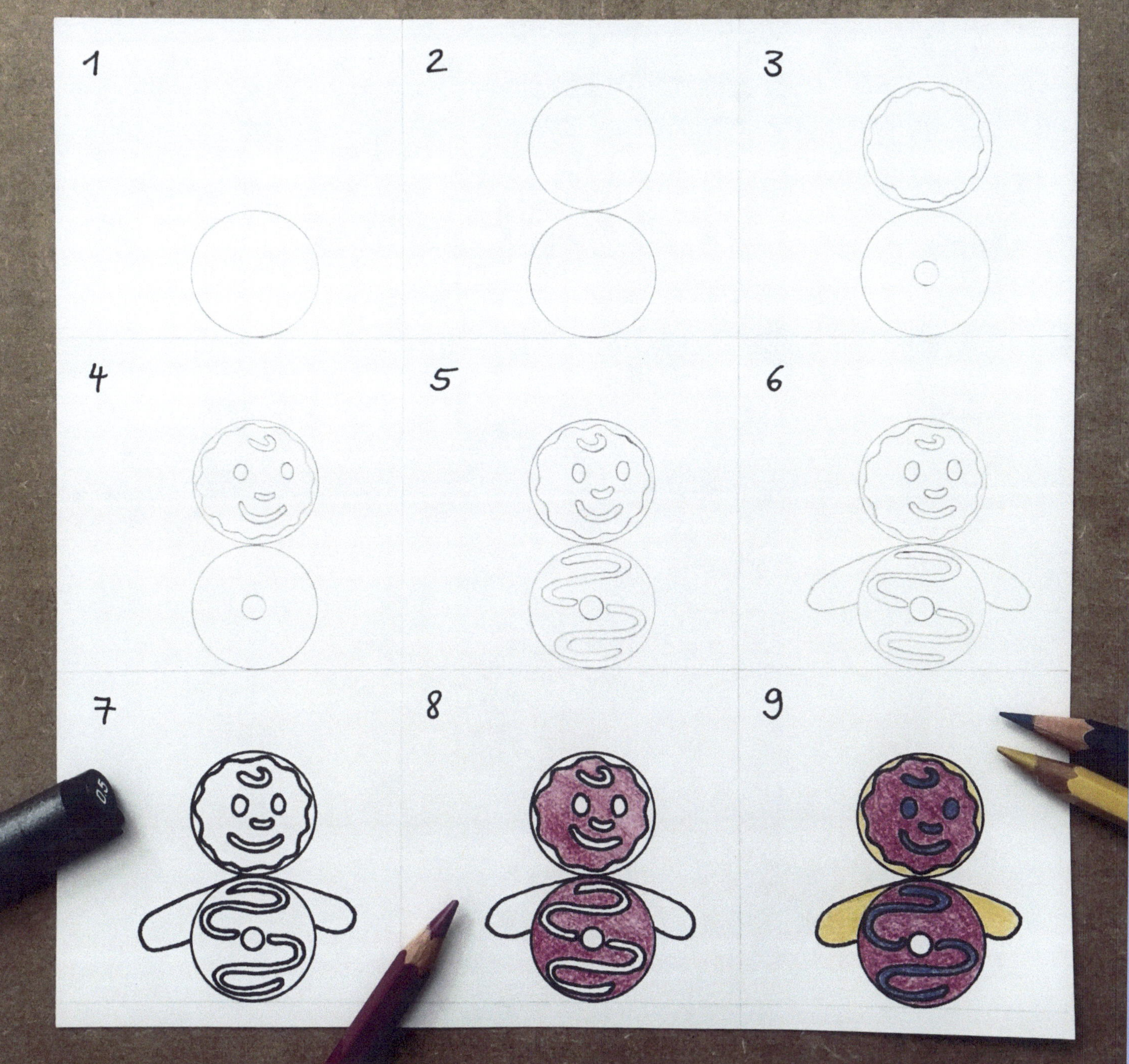

Deleted Lines

"A Snowman stood day in, day out,
In front of my little gingerbread house.

One morning though, alas, my Dear,
The Snowman has suddenly disappeared!

Where could he be? Where did he go?
What's he doing all alone?

I can't find him anywhere,
(???) ... "

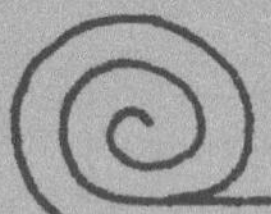

"Well, it could be that he just felt,
That too long on this spot he dwelled.

It seems like it, 'cause soon thereafter,
He wrote to me, my … (???).

He's doing well, he loves the new,
The mountains here are pretty too,

It's just the heights, he's not used to,
… (???) "

"The horseman knows a destination,
The circus tent next to the station.

The Circus is my Snowman's dream,
Of course, we go there … (???)"

"We plan a little city tour,
The Eiffel Tower … (???) "

"We'd like to meet the Bedouins,
Out in the desert … (???)"

"Now once upon a distant time
I had a journey on my mind."

"The final house is made of scraps,
I'm making sure it won't collapse."

"Just for the final storybook,
I'll add some colour for the look."

(Book cover:)
"Follow my Snowman on his journey from
gingerbread house to storybook."

MY SNOWMAN
GOES ON A JOURNEY

Colour your Storybook

Amanda S. Mosaic

ISBN 978-3-948493-02-8

MY SNOWMAN
ENJOYS THE SUMMER

Colour your Storybook

Amanda S. Mosaic

ISBN 978-3-948493-06-6

MY SNOWMAN
AT THE MAKER FAIRE

Colour your Storybook

Amanda S. Mosaic

ISBN 978-3-948493-10-3

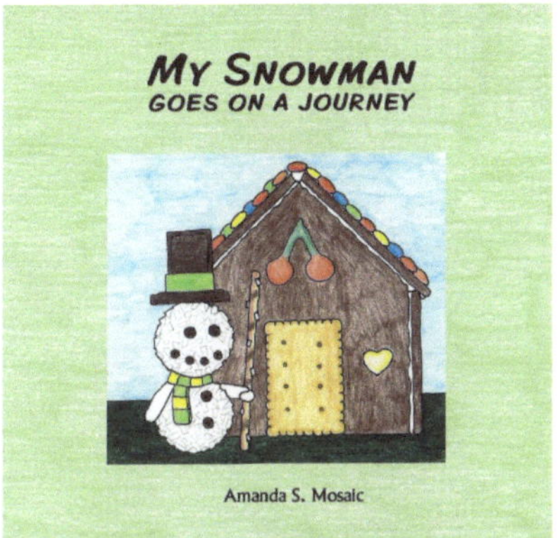

MY SNOWMAN
GOES ON A JOURNEY

Amanda S. Mosaic

ISBN 978-3-948493-03-5

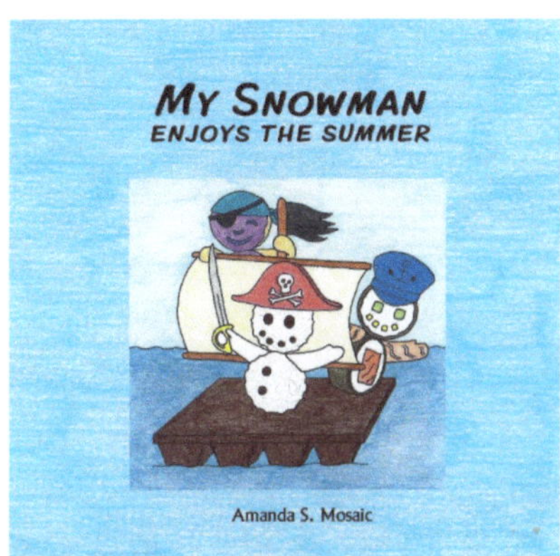

MY SNOWMAN
ENJOYS THE SUMMER

Amanda S. Mosaic

ISBN 978-3-948493-07-3

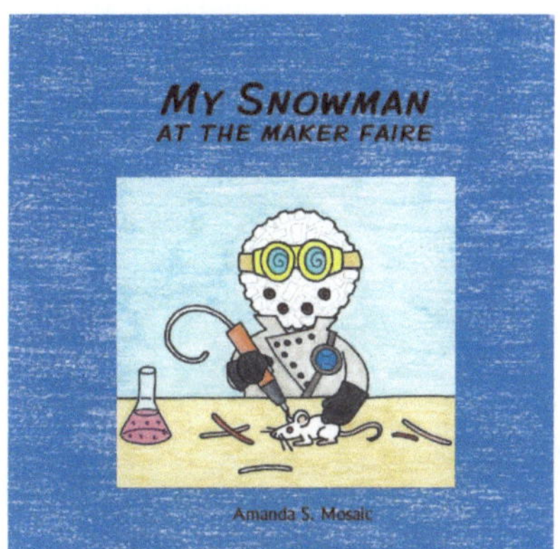

MY SNOWMAN
AT THE MAKER FAIRE

Amanda S. Mosaic

ISBN 978-3-948493-11-0

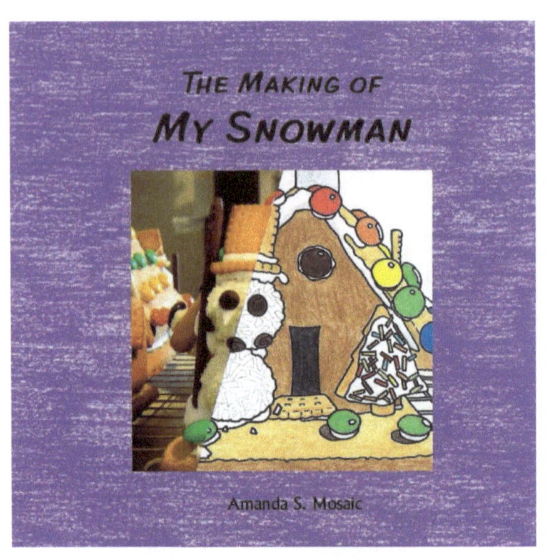

ISBN 978-3-948493-13-4

ISBN 978-3-948493-12-7

WWW.AMANDASMOSAIC.COM

ISBN 978-3-948493-00-4

ISBN 978-3-948493-01-1

ISBN 978-3-948493-04-2

ISBN 978-3-948493-05-9

ISBN 978-3-948493-08-0

ISBN 978-3-948493-09-7